The
Story Girl

Book 1

D0684613

From the author of Anne of Green Gables

L.M. Montgomery

Ward County Public Library

The Story Girl
Book 1 ™

DISCARDED

THE KING COUSINS

Adapted by Barbara Davoll

Zonderkidz

Zonder**kidz**.

The children's group of Zondervan

www.zonderkidz.com

The King Cousins
© 2004 The Zondervan Corporation, David Macdonald, trustee and
Ruth Macdonald

Requests for information should be addressed to:
Grand Rapids, Michigan 49530

Library of Congress Cataloging-in-Publication Data

Montgomery, L. M. (Lucy Maud), 1874-1942.
  The King cousins / L.M. Montgomery ; adaptation written by
  Barbara Davoll.
    p. cm. - - (The story girl ; bk. 1)
Summary: Two boys arrive for a visit with relatives on Prince Edward
  Island and have adventures involving a boy's first visit to church, raising
  funds for a school library, and a miser willing to pay for one of Sara
  Stanley's captivating stories.
    ISBN 0-310-70598-3 (pbk. ; alk. paper)
    [1. Storytellers—Fiction.   2. Cousins—Fiction.   3. Prince Edward
  Island—Fiction.] I. Davoll, Barbara. II. Title
PZ7.M768Ki 2004
  {Fic}—dc21   2003001056

"*The Story Girl*" and "*L. M. Montgomery*" are trademarks of Heirs of L. M.
Montgomery Inc., used under license by The Zondervan Corporation.

"*The King Cousins*" is adapted from "*The Story Girl*" by L. M. Montgomery.
Adaptation authorized by David Macdonald, trustee, and Ruth Macdonald, the
heirs of L. M. Montgomery.

Photograph of L. M. Montgomery used by permission of L. M. Montgomery
Collection, Archival and Special Collections, University of Guelph Library.

All rights reserved. No part of this publication may be reproduced, stored in
a retrieval system, or transmitted in any form or by any means—electronic,
mechanical, photocopy, recording, or any other—except for brief quotations
in printed reviews, without the prior permission of the publisher.

Zonderkidz is a trademark of Zondervan

Editor: Gwen Ellis
Interior design: Susan Ambs
Art direction: Laura Maitner

04 05 06 07/❖OP/ 10 9 8 7 6 5 4 3 2 1

Contents

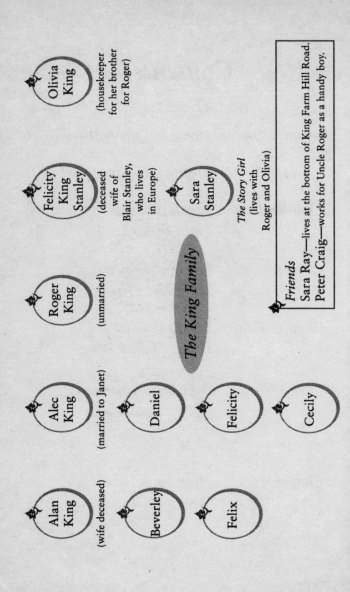

The King Family

Olivia King
(housekeeper for her brother for Roger)

Felicity King Stanley
(deceased wife of Blair Stanley, who lives in Europe)

Sara Stanley
The Story Girl
(lives with Roger and Olivia)

Roger King
(unmarried)

Alec King
(married to Janet)

Daniel

Felicity

Cecily

Alan King
(wife deceased)

Beverley

Felix

Friends
Sara Ray—lives at the bottom of King Farm Hill Road.
Peter Craig—works for Uncle Roger as a handy boy.

Home of Our Fathers

"I do like a road, because you are always wondering what is at the end of it."

Chapter One

The Story Girl said that once upon a time. My brother, Felix, and I had not heard her say it yet, but we were wondering about the road ahead of us on the May morning when we left Toronto. We stood with Father and our housekeeper, Mrs. MacLaren, on the platform at the Toronto train station. Felix and I bounced up and down with excitement. There it was—the train that would take us to the coast where we would catch the ferry to Prince Edward Island! The engineer blew the whistle as the engine came around the curve toward us.

It seemed almost too good to be true. Finally we were going to see the Island where Father had grown up. He had told us so much about it. Soon we would meet our cousins Felicity, Cecily, and Dan. They lived on the old King homestead. Sara Stanley, another cousin of ours, was living on the Island, too. Since her mother died, she had been living with Uncle Roger and Aunt Olivia on a farm next to the King's place.

It was Sara who was called "the Story Girl." We assumed we'd find out soon why she had been given that name. Aunt Olivia's letters about her and the other cousins were always funny, describing all the good times they had together. We couldn't wait to get on the train as it chugged slowly up to the platform.

When Father first told us we were going to the King farm for the summer, we tried not to show too much excitement. Father was sorry he could not go with us to his old home. He had to go to South America to take charge of a new office there. It was a great opportunity for Father that included a promotion and a pay raise. The only problem was he couldn't take us with him right then. Mother had died before we were old enough to remember her, so that meant there would be no one in Toronto to take care of us. In the end, Father decided to send us to our relatives on Prince Edward Island until he could find a home for us in South America.

After bear hugs from Father and a promise to write each week, we were bustled onto the train by Mrs. MacLaren. It was her job to deliver us to Uncle Alec, another of Father's brothers. We would stay at his farm for the summer.

We must have been a handful on the trip. As we were pulling our baggage from the cart, we heard Mrs. MacLaren telling Uncle Alec: "The fat one isn't so bad. He doesn't move as fast and get out of your sight like the thin one can. The only safe way to travel with those young boys would be to have them both tied to you with a short rope—a mighty short rope."

The "fat one" was Felix, and he was very sensitive about his plumpness. He was always doing exercises to try to thin down, but it seemed he always just gained more weight. He said he didn't care, but he *did*—he cared very much. He frowned at Mrs. MacLaren when she said that. He hadn't liked her since the day she told him he would soon be as broad as he was long. I felt sorry when we said good-bye to her. But by the time we reached the open country, both of us had forgotten all about her. We drove along happily, enjoying Uncle Alec's company. Felix and I loved him from the first moment we met.

Uncle Alec was a small man with thin, delicate features, a close-clipped gray beard, and large, tired blue eyes. He looked just like Father. It was obvious right from the start that Uncle Alec liked children and was glad to welcome "Alan's boys." We felt right at home with him and were not afraid to ask him questions on any subject that came to our minds. By the time we had traveled the twenty-four miles to his house on the King homestead, the three of us had become good friends.

It was dark when we reached Carlisle. We couldn't see much of anything as we drove up the lane to the old King homestead on the hill near the town. Behind us a young moon was hanging over the meadow. All was peaceful in the soft, moist shadows of the May night, as we peered eagerly through the darkness.

"Look, there's the big willow tree, Bev," Felix said as he punched me in the ribs. Bev is my name. It's short for Beverley. And don't you dare laugh. I know it's an unusual name for a boy. But I didn't have anything to do with choosing a name for myself.

I looked where Felix was pointing and sure enough there it was—the tree Grandfather King had planted by accident when he stuck a willow stick in the ground and it grew. We had heard stories from our father about how he and our aunts and uncles played in the shadow of that same big tree. *I'm going to climb it tomorrow*, I thought.

As we continued up the lane toward the King homestead, we saw the old orchard on our right. Father had told us about that, too. And on the left was the big white farmhouse. A friendly light shone out through an open door. In the doorway was Aunt Janet, a big bustling woman with full-blown rosy cheeks. She'd come to welcome us.

Walking into the kitchen where we would soon have supper, we saw huge hams and slabs of bacon hung from the low, dark ceiling rafters. The kitchen was such a pleasant place that we felt at home right away. We sat across the table from Felicity, Cecily, and Dan—the cousins we had just met. All three of them stared at us when they thought we were busy eating. And both of us stared right back at them when we thought they wouldn't notice. We spent the whole meal catching each other at the staring game and feeling embarrassed.

Dan was the oldest of Uncle Alec's children—thirteen—and was a lean, freckled fellow with long, straight brown hair and the shapely King nose. The Kings were noted for two things about their looks—their noses and their complexions. Dan's mouth, on the other hand, was long and narrow and twisted and not at all attractive. But he grinned in a friendly fashion. Later when Felix and I talked about Dan, we both thought we were going to like him.

Next was Felicity. She was twelve and had been named after Aunt Felicity, our cousin Sara's mother, who was now buried in the old Carlisle graveyard. Cousin Felicity, we had been told, was known as the beauty of the family. When we met her, we were not disappointed. She had lovely dark-blue eyes, soft, feathery golden curls, and the famous pink and white King complexion. Felicity looked adorable in a pink print dress and a frilly apron. Dan said she had "dressed up" in honor of our coming. No girl had ever gone to the trouble of dressing up for us—we felt very important.

Eleven-year-old Cecily was pretty also—or would have been had Felicity not been there. Compared to Felicity all other girls looked pale and thin. But Cecily's hair was smooth and brown and had a satiny shine. Her mild brown eyes had just a hint of shyness in them.

We remembered that Aunt Olivia had said in a letter that Cecily took after the Ward side of the family and that she had no sense of humor. We didn't know what that meant, but we didn't think it was a compliment. Still, we both thought we might like Cecily better than Felicity. Felicity seemed uppity and a little too aware of her good looks. Well . . . to put it bluntly, she seemed like a snob.

"It's a wonder the Story Girl hasn't come over to see you yet," said Uncle Alec. "She's been very excited about your coming."

"Who is the Story Girl?" asked Felix, for at that point, we had not been told.

"Oh, Sara—Sara Stanley. We call her the Story Girl partly because she tells such wonderful stories and also because there is a girl named Sara Ray, who lives at the foot of the hill. She often comes up to play with us. It's awkward to have two girls with the same name. Besides, Sara Stanley doesn't care for her name. She'd rather be called the Story Girl."

"She hasn't been well all day," explained Cecily. "Aunt Olivia wouldn't let her come out in the night

14

air. She was very disappointed when she had to go to bed instead."

Then Dan, speaking for the first time, said Peter had also been intending to come over but had to go on an errand for his mother.

"Who's Peter?" we asked.

Uncle Alec answered, "He is Uncle Roger and Aunt Olivia's hired handy boy. His name is Peter Craig. He is a real smart boy with lots of mischief in him."

"He wants to be Felicity's boyfriend," said Dan with a sly look at his sister.

"Don't be silly, Dan." Aunt Janet spoke a little more severely than she had intended.

Felicity tossed her golden head and shot a withering glance at her brother. "I wouldn't have a hired boy for a boyfriend," she protested with her nose in the air. She was angry. Evidently she didn't care for Peter, and she was not about to be linked with anyone she considered beneath her. I was beginning to form an opinion about my hoity-toity cousin, and it wasn't pleasant. I wondered what she thought about us—the intruders from Toronto.

We wanted our cousins to like us, but at the moment, I was too tired to worry about it very much. When it was time to go to bed, we were quite willing. Aunt Janet whisked us away upstairs to the very room that had once been Father's. It overlooked the grove of pine trees and was Dan's room now. He slept in his own bed in a corner opposite from ours. On our beds were sweet-smelling sheets and pillows, and each of us had one of Grandmother King's patchwork quilts to cover us.

Through the open window, we heard the frogs singing down in the swamp near Brook Meadow. We had heard frogs sing in Ontario, of course, but it seemed that the Prince Edward Island frogs were more tuneful and mellow. Or was it simply that all the tales we had heard were lending their magic? All the sights and sounds around us made those frogs' songs sound different.

This was Father's home—and now for a time, it was going to be our home! Here under the roof built by our great-grandfather King ninety years ago, we felt cozy and at home. We had not felt that way since our mother died.

"Just think, those are the very frogs Father listened to when he was a little boy," whispered Felix.

"They can hardly be the same frogs," I whispered back. "It's been twenty years since Father left here."

"Well, they're descendants of the frogs he heard," said Felix, "and they're singing in the same swamp. That's close enough for me."

Across the narrow hall was the girls' room. Through our open bedroom door, we could hear

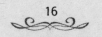

them laughing and talking as they got ready for bed. They were talking more loudly than they might have if they had realized how far their voices would carry.

"What do you think of the boys?" asked Cecily.

"Beverley is handsome, but Felix is too fat," answered Felicity promptly.

Felix rolled over and grunted in disgust. I began to think more kindly about Felicity. *She can't be all bad,* I thought. *It might not be altogether her fault she is so full of pride. How can she help but feel good when she looks in the mirror?*

"I think they're both fun and good-looking," said Cecily.

Well, that's nice, I thought. I was glad for what she had said, and I hoped Felix had heard it, too.

"I wonder what the Story Girl will think of them?" said Cecily, as if that were the most important thing.

Somehow we thought it was important, too. We felt that if the Story Girl didn't approve of us, it made little difference who else did.

Felix spoke up from his bed. "I wonder if the Story Girl is pretty?"

"No, she isn't," said Dan instantly, from across the room. "But you'll think she is while she's talking to you. Everybody does. It's only when you go away from her that you find out she isn't pretty after all."

The girls' door shut with a bang. Silence fell over the house. We drifted into the land of sleep, wondering if the Story Girl would like us.

Meeting the Story Girl

*If voices had color, hers would have been a
rainbow. It made words live.*

Chapter Two

We woke up early the next morning, soon after the sun was up. The May sunshine was just beginning to peep through our window. A gentle spring wind blew through the feathery branches of the pine trees.

We slipped out of bed and dressed without waking Dan. He was still sleeping with his mouth open and his bedclothes kicked off. Everything was very still as we crept downstairs. We could hear someone in the kitchen rattling the stove. *Probably Uncle Alec building a fire,* I thought. We stopped for a moment in front of the old grandfather clock in the hall. We had never seen one before and thought its mechanism very interesting.

"Look Bev!" my brother exclaimed. "Here are the marks Father made on it." Sure enough, the little door of the clock had a dent in it just as Father had told us. He had kicked it in anger once when he was a little boy. "He must have been *really* mad!" Felix said.

We quietly opened the front door and stepped out into the early morning beauty of Prince Edward

Island. Uncle Roger's house was on the other side of the pine trees that lined the driveway. Father lived there with his younger sister—our Aunt Olivia—and our cousin Sara Stanley. The path that led to their home seemed to have an air of mystery about it.

To the right was the famous King orchard, where Grandfather King had planted the first trees sixty years earlier, soon after he and Grandmother were married. I will never forget the wonderful smell of apple blossoms and blooming plum, cherry, and pear trees. To this day, when I get a whiff of blossoming fruit trees, I am reminded of that place. We knew that all of the fourteen King children had "birth" trees that had been planted in the orchard when they were born. The grandchildren also had trees named in their honor. Father had told us that important visitors to the homestead had trees named for them, too. We were anxious to find our trees.

There was a whitewashed gate that led to the orchard. Just as we reached it and were ready to explore, we noticed a girl. She and a gray cat were standing in the lane that led to Uncle Roger's house. She waved to us and smiled a friendly smile. We knew she must be Sara Stanley, the Story Girl.

As we drew closer, we saw that she was just as Dan had said. She was tall for her fourteen years, slim and straight. Her dark-brown curls were tied in a clever way with red ribbons that framed her long face. Although her mouth seemed a little large for her face, she had bright hazel eyes that were interesting. But no—she wasn't pretty.

Then she said, "Good morning."

We had never heard a voice like hers. I cannot describe it. I might say it was clear; I might say it was sweet. I might say it was lovely and bell-like. All of those things would be true, but they would not give you a true idea of the sound of the Story Girl's voice.

If voices had color, hers would have been a rainbow. It made words live. We instantly felt when she spoke that it *was* a good morning—the very best morning that had ever happened in this wonderful world.

"You must be Felix and Beverley," she said. She was so different from Felicity and Cecily. From that moment on, we were like good friends who had known each other for a hundred years.

"I am very glad to see you. I was so disappointed I couldn't go to your house last night, so I got up early this morning. I felt sure you would be up early too and that you'd like to have me tell you some things about the homestead or the Island. I can tell things so much better than Felicity or Cecily. Do you think Felicity is *very* pretty?"

"She's the prettiest girl I ever saw," I said, remembering that Felicity had called me handsome.

"The boys all think so," answered the Story Girl. "And I suppose she is. She is a great cook too, even though she is only twelve. I can't cook. I'm trying to learn, but I don't have the knack for it. Aunt Olivia doesn't think I'll ever do much in the kitchen. But I'd love to be able to make pies and cakes as well as Felicity does. Even though she can cook, she is sometimes a pain. Cecily is ever so much more clever. Cecily's a dear friend. Uncle Alec and Aunt Janet are nice, too."

"What is Aunt Olivia like?" asked Felix.

"Aunt Olivia is very pretty. She is just like a pansy—all velvety and purply and goldy."

Felix and I could just imagine a velvet, purple-and-gold–pansy woman as the Story Girl spoke.

"But is she nice?" I asked. That was the main question about grown-ups. Their looks didn't matter.

"She is lovely, but she is getting old—twenty-nine you know. I like Aunt Olivia because she says children should just be left to grow up. She is ever so much fun. Aunt Janet complains all the time that I'm not being brought up as a proper young lady, but I think I'll do all right. I love living with Uncle Roger and Aunt Olivia."

"What is Uncle Roger like?" was our next question.

Ward County Public Library

"Well, I like Uncle Roger. He is big and jolly, but he teases people too much. You ask him a serious question and you get a silly answer. He hardly ever scolds or gets cross though, and *that* is something. He's just an old bachelor."

"Do you think he'll ever get married?" asked Felix.

"I don't know. Aunt Olivia wishes he would because she's tired of keeping house for him. She thinks he never will, though, because he's looking for a perfect wife. She says that since he isn't perfect himself, he'll never find a woman to have *him*."

"This isn't Topsy, is it?" I asked, petting the cat. The moment I asked I knew at once the question was foolish. Topsy, the cat Father had as a boy, would have been more than thirty years old. No cat has that many lives.

"No, but it is Topsy's great-great-great-grandson," answered the Story Girl seriously. "His name is Paddy, and he belongs to me. We have barn cats, but Paddy never associates with them. He just follows me around like a shadow. Oh, I am so glad you boys have come. We were short of boys, you know—only Dan and Peter to four girls."

"*Four girls?* Oh, yes—Sara Ray. What is she like?"

"She lives just down the hill. She's only eleven and her mother is very strict. She never allows Sara to do anything—not even read a story. Sara always feels bad when she does things her mother doesn't want her to do. It's hard for all of us. Her mother's rules never stop Sara from doing things—it just spoils her fun. Sara is pale and nervous and thin. I think it's because her mother will never allow her to have a snack. Not that her mother is mean. She just thinks snacks aren't healthy. Isn't it fortunate we weren't born into that kind of family? When I think it all over, I'm really thankful that Grandfather and Grandmother King married each other. There were so many other people they might have married."

Felix and I shivered. It took the Story Girl to help us know the dreadful danger of being born as someone else.

"Who lives over there?" I asked, pointing to a house across the fields.

"Oh, that belongs to a man by the name of Jasper Dale, but everybody calls him the Awkward Man. They say he writes poetry. He never goes out much because he's so clumsy. He's always falling over his own feet. The girls laugh at him, and he doesn't like it. I'll tell you a story about him sometime."

"Look, do you see a road just beyond the Awkward Man's house? That road leads over to Green Gables. That's where another grown-up cousin lives. Her name is Anne Shirley, and she is quite a lady.

She is away taking some summer studies at college right now. She's going to be a teacher. I hope you get to meet her sometime, she is a lot of fun."

Across the valley we could see a little gray roof. "That's old Peg Bowen's house. She's weird. In the winter, she stays inside with a lot of pet animals. In the summer, she goes all over the country and begs for her meals. Grown-ups have always told us that if we aren't good, Peg Bowen will catch us. I'm not afraid of her anymore, but just the same, I don't think I'd like her to catch me. Sara Ray is very frightened of her.

It was a May morning and we said we'd like to visit the orchard.

"All right. I know some wonderful stories about it," she said as we walked across the yard. Paddy, who was twitching his tail, followed us.

The latch of the gate clicked under the Story Girl's hand, and the next moment, we were inside the King orchard.

"It's all just as Father described it," said Felix with a happy sigh. "There's the well with the Chinese roof."

We hurried over to it. The very deep well was one Uncle Stephen had built when he returned from China.

"There's a cup just like the one that used to be here in Father's time!" exclaimed Felix. He was pointing to an old-fashioned cup of faded blue china that sat on a little shelf near the well.

"It is the very *same* cup," said the Story Girl with emphasis. "Isn't it amazing? That cup has been here forty years, and it's never been broken. Hundreds of people have drunk from it."

We took a drink from the blue cup and then went to find our birthday trees. We were disappointed to find that they were large, mature trees. It seemed to us that they should still be young trees, since we were still young boys.

"The apples from your tree are lovely to eat," the Story Girl said to me. "But the apples on Felix's tree are only good for pies."

"That's all right by me. I like pies," said Felix. "And I like to hear you talk," he added in his serious, stuffy way.

"Everybody does," responded the Story Girl coolly. "I'm glad you like the way I talk. But I want you to like *me, too*. At least as well as you like Felicity and Cecily—not *better*. I wanted that once but I got over it. I found out in Sunday school, the day the minister taught our class, that it was selfish to want people to like you *better* than someone else. But I want you to like me just the same as you like the other girls."

"Well, I will for sure," said Felix confidently. I think he was remembering that Felicity had called him fat.

Cecily then joined us. It was Felicity's morning to help prepare breakfast, so she couldn't come. We all went to "Uncle Stephen's walk." He was our uncle who died as a sailor in a terrible storm at sea. His "walk" was a double row of apple trees planted as a memorial to him.

From his walk, we went to the Pulpit Stone. It was a huge, gray rock, as high as a man's head. It was straight and smooth in front and had natural steps in back that sloped down behind. There was a ledge in the middle of it where you could stand. This was where the aunts and uncles acted out plays and gave concerts and speeches. From here, Uncle Edward, the preacher in the family, had preached his first sermon at the age of eight.

The Story Girl climbed onto the ledge, sat on the rim, and looked at us. Paddy daintily washed his face with his paws.

"Now for your stories about the orchard," I said expectantly.

"There are two important ones: *The Poet Who Was Kissed* and *The Tale of the Family Ghost*. Which one would you like to hear?" the Story Girl asked.

"Tell them both," said Felix greedily, "but tell the ghost one first."

Legends of the Old Orchard

⤜⤛

*"I love a flower garden. I think
I could always be good if I lived
in a garden all the time."*

Chapter Three

I shuddered when my brother, Felix, asked the Story Girl to tell the ghost story first. I wasn't sure I wanted to hear it just then—at least not *first*. Even the Story Girl herself looked uncertain.

"That story should be told at night in the shadows," she replied. "Then it would frighten the souls out of your bodies."

We weren't sure we wanted the souls frightened out of our bodies. "Ghost stories are more comfortable in the daytime," said Felix.

The Story Girl began, and we listened wide-eyed. Cecily listened just as eagerly as we did, though she had heard it many times before.

"Long, long ago," began the Story Girl, "even before Grandfather King was born, an orphan cousin lived with Grandfather's parents. Her name was Emily King. She was very small and sweet. Her soft brown eyes were too timid to look straight at anybody, kind of like Cecily's. And she had long shiny brown curls like mine. She had a tiny birthmark like a pink butterfly on one cheek—right here.

"Of course there was no orchard back then, but there were some white birch trees. Emily liked to sit among the birches and read or sew. She had a gentleman friend, whose name was Malcolm Ward. He was as handsome as a prince. She loved him with all her heart, and he loved her, too. But they had never spoken of their love for each other. They used to meet under the birches and talk about everything—except love.

"One day he told her he was coming the next day to ask her a very important question. He said he would look for her under the birches when he came. Emily eagerly promised to meet him there. She knew exactly what question he wanted to ask, and she desperately wanted to become his wife.

"The next day she dressed herself beautifully in her best pale-blue muslin dress. She had never been happier as she went to the birches with a smile on her face and every curl in place. While she was waiting there thinking lovely thoughts, a neighbor boy came running up. This neighbor boy, who didn't know about Emily's feelings for Malcolm, cried out 'Malcolm Ward has been accidentally shot and killed with his own gun.'

"Emily put her hands over her heart—like this— and fell, all white and broken under the birches. When she awoke from her faint, she didn't cry. But she was changed. Every day she dressed herself in her blue dress and sat waiting under the birches. She became paler and weaker as time passed. But oddly enough, the pink butterfly on her cheek grew redder. It was said that when the winter came, she died of a broken heart. People say that sometimes they think they can see her even yet sitting under the trees. That is why we call her 'the family ghost.'"

"I wouldn't want to see her," said Cecily with a shudder. "I'd be afraid."

"There isn't anything to be afraid of," said the Story Girl. "It's not as if it's a strange ghost. It's our own family ghost. So, of course, it won't hurt us."

Felix and I were glad we hadn't heard the tale in the evening. We hadn't heard many ghost stories and thought it probably wasn't real. But the Story Girl had sure made it *seem* real to us. Looking back toward the house, we saw Felicity running toward us, her curls flying out behind her like a cloud.

"Is breakfast ready, Felicity?" called the Story Girl. "Do I still have time to tell the boys the story of *The Poet Who Was Kissed?*"

"Breakfast is ready, but we can't have it 'til Father comes in from the barn. You'll have time," said Felicity, her eyes shining and her cheeks rosy from running. She sat down on the grass with us, arranging her skirt and apron just so. Felix and I couldn't keep our eyes off her. Her young beauty was breathtaking. But when the Story Girl spoke again, we forgot to look at Felicity. We hung on every word as Sara began to spin another tale.

"About ten years after Grandfather and Grandmother King were married, a young man came to visit them. He was a distant relative of Grandmother's and a poet, who would one day become famous. He came into the orchard to write a poem and fell asleep with his head on a bench that used to be under Grandfather's tree.

"Then Great-Aunt Edith came into the orchard. (Of course, she was not a great-aunt then for she was only eighteen.) She was beautiful with red lips and jet-black hair and eyes. They say she was always full of mischief. She had been away and didn't know about the poet. But when she saw him sleeping there, she thought he was the cousin they had been expecting from Scotland. She tiptoed up to him, bent over, and kissed his cheek.

"When he opened his big blue eyes and looked up into Edith's face, she blushed as red as a rose. She knew this man could not be her cousin from Scotland. Her cousin had black eyes. Edith ran away and hid; and of course, she felt still worse when she learned that the man was a famous poet. But the poet wrote one of his most beautiful poems about it afterward and sent it to her. It was published in one of his books."

We had seen it all through Sara's musical words—the sleeping poet and our embarrassed great-aunt. We had almost felt the kiss drop as lightly as a rose petal on his cheek. "They should have been married," said Felix.

"Well, in a book they would have been, but you see, this was real life," said Sara. "We sometimes act the story out. I like it best when Peter plays the poet, but we can hardly ever coax him to play the part—except when Felicity plays Edith. I don't like it when Dan is the poet because he is so freckled and screws his eyes up tight."

"What is Peter like?" I asked.

"Peter is fun. His mother is a washer lady who lives on Markdale Road. Peter's father ran away and left them when Peter was only three years old. His father hasn't come back, and they don't know if he is alive or dead. Isn't that a nice way to treat your family? Peter has worked for a living ever since he was six years old. Uncle Roger sends him to school in the winter and pays him wages in the summer. We all like Peter—except for Felicity."

"I like Peter well enough in his place," said Felicity in a snobby way. "But you make too much of him. Mother says he is only a hired boy who hasn't been brought up well. I don't think you should make an equal of him like you do."

Laughter rippled over the Story Girl's face. "Peter is a real gentleman, and he is more interesting than *you* could ever be if you were educated for a hundred years," she snipped at Felicity.

"He can hardly write," said Felicity.

"William the Conqueror couldn't write at all," said the Story Girl.

"He never goes to church, and he never says his prayers," retorted Felicity.

"I do too," said Peter himself, appearing through a little gap in the orchard hedge. "I say my prayers sometimes."

Peter was a handsome young man with thick black curls—and he was barefoot. He wore the same thing every day, like a uniform. But the faded, plaid shirt and pair of old corduroy knickers (knee-length pants) looked great on him. He wore his clothing with pride and was so cute that he seemed much better dressed than he really was.

"You don't pray very often," accused Felicity.

"Well, God probably listens to me more since I don't pester him all the time," argued Peter.

Felicity's mouth curled in scorn at this remark. "You never go to church anyhow," she said. She was determined not to be argued down.

"Well, I ain't going to church 'til I've made up my mind whether I'm going to be a Methodist or a Presbyterian. Aunt Jane was a Methodist. My mother ain't much of anything, but I mean to be something. It's more respectable to be a Methodist or a Presbyterian or *something* than not to be anything."

"That's not the same as being *born* something," said Felicity with her nose in the air.

"I think it's a good deal better to pick your own religion than to *have* to take it just because it's what your folks have," retorted Peter.

"Never mind quarreling," said Cecily. "You leave Peter alone, Felicity. Peter, meet Beverley and Felix King, our cousins. We are all going to be good friends and have a great summer. Oh look! I see Father coming from the barn. Let's go have some of Felicity's nice breakfast."

Felix and I looked at each other with questions in our eyes. This talk about church was something we had never considered. I was glad it was time to eat—that at least was something we could all agree on. It seemed it would be an interesting summer for sure.

On the way to the house, the Story Girl asked Peter what he was going to do that day. "Oh, plow the field out back and dig your Aunt Olivia's flower beds."

"Aunt Olivia and I planted the sweet peas yesterday," said the Story Girl, "and I planted a little flower bed of my own. I am *not* going to dig them up this year to see if they've sprouted like I did last year. I'm going to try to have patience no matter how long they take."

"I'm going to help mother plant the vegetable garden today," said Felicity.

"Oh, I never like the vegetable garden," said the Story Girl. "Except when I'm hungry. Then I *do* like to go and look at the nice little rows of onions and beets. But I love a flower garden. I think I could always be good if I lived in a garden all the time."

"Adam and Eve lived in a garden all the time," said Felicity, "and they weren't always good."

"They might not have been good as long as they were if they hadn't lived in a garden," said the Story Girl.

Peter, the Story Girl, and Paddy, the cat, slipped through the gap in the hedge to go to their own home for breakfast. The rest of us walked on toward the house.

"So what do you think of the Story Girl?" asked Felicity.

"She's just fine," said Felix with enthusiasm. "I never heard anyone tell stories like she does."

"She can't cook," said Felicity, "and she doesn't have a good complexion. And, listen to *this*. She says she's going to be an *actress* when she grows up. Isn't that *dreadful!*"

We said we didn't exactly see why that would be so bad.

"Oh, because actresses are *always* wicked people," answered Felicity in a shocked tone. "I think she will be one as soon as she can. Her father will back her in it. He is an *artist*, you know."

Evidently Felicity thought all artists and actresses were poor trash.

"Aunt Olivia says the Story Girl is fascinating," said Cecily.

What a word! *Fascinating*! It described her perfectly.

Dan did not come down until breakfast was over. Aunt Janet scolded him so harshly that we were embarrassed. Her scolding made us decide to stay on her good side. We sure wouldn't want her to come after us for anything. But all in all, the summer seemed promising. With the Story Girl to tell us wonderful stories, Felicity to look at, Cecily to admire us, Dan and Peter to play with, what more could we want?

The Wedding Veil of the Proud Princess

"It doesn't matter which you are—Methodist or Presbyterian," reasoned the Story Girl. "They both can go to heaven."

Chapter Four

By the time we had lived in Carlisle a couple of weeks, we felt as though we belonged and had all the freedom the other kids enjoyed. We were great friends with our cousins and with Peter. Even the mousy Sara Ray, who lived down the hill, was our good friend.

We went to school (on Prince Edward Island, school went into the summer) and took care of the home chores assigned to us. But we still had long hours for play. Even Peter had plenty of spare time when the planting was over. We had some differences of opinion, but for the most part, we got along very well. As for the grown-ups, they suited us also.

We adored Aunt Olivia. She was pretty, lots of fun, and very kind. If we kept ourselves fairly clean and didn't quarrel or talk slang, Aunt Olivia didn't bother us. Aunt Janet, on the other hand, gave us too much good advice. She was constantly telling us not to do one thing or another. We couldn't remember half of her instructions.

Uncle Roger was just as the Story Girl had described him—lots of fun and full of teasing. We liked him, but sometimes we felt like he was making fun of us. We didn't like that in him. We loved Uncle Alec though and felt we always had a friend in him.

The social life of Carlisle centered on Sunday school. We were especially interested in it, because our teacher made the lessons so interesting. We no longer thought attendance at church was disagreeable. Instead we looked forward to it with pleasure and tried to do what the teacher taught us. At least we tried hard to do right on Mondays and Tuesdays. We didn't always remember to do right as the rest of the week rolled by.

Our teacher was deeply interested in missions. One of her talks on the subject inspired the Story Girl with a desire to do some home missionary work on her own. The only thing she could think of, though, was to try to get Peter to go to church.

Felicity didn't approve and said so plainly. "He won't know how to behave, for he's never been inside a church in his life," she warned. "He'll do something awful, and then you'll feel ashamed and wish you'd never asked him to go. We'll all be disgraced! It's all right to take up money for the heathen and send missionaries to them. They're far away, and we don't have to associate with them. But I don't want to sit in a pew with a hired boy."

The Story Girl didn't pay any attention and continued to coax the unwilling Peter. It was not easy. Peter did not come from a churchgoing family. And besides, he had not made up his mind whether he wanted to be a Presbyterian or a Methodist.

"It doesn't matter which you are—Methodist or Presbyterian," reasoned the Story Girl. "They both can go to heaven."

"But one way must be easier or better than the other or else there would only be one kind," argued Peter. "I want to find the easiest way. And I've got a hankering after the Methodists. My Aunt Jane was a Methodist."

"Isn't she one still?" asked saucy Felicity.

"Well, I don't know exactly. She's dead," replied Peter. "Do people go on being just the same after they're dead?"

"No, of course not. They're not anything then. They're just saints—that is, if they go to heaven."

"S'posen they go to the other place?" asked Peter.

Felicity had no answer for that. She turned her back on Peter and walked away. The Story Girl returned to her argument.

"We have such a lovely minister, Peter. He looks just like the picture of Saint John that Father sent me, only he is old and his hair is white. I know you'd like him. And even if you were going to be a

Methodist, it wouldn't hurt you to go to the Presbyterian church. The nearest Methodist church is over at Markdale, and you can't go there now. Go to the Presbyterian with us until you're old enough to have a horse and go to Markdale."

"But s'posen I get too fond of being Presbyterian and can't change if I want to," objected Peter.

Altogether the Story Girl had a hard time of it with Peter. But one day she came to us with the announcement that Peter had decided to go to church. We were out in Uncle Roger's hill pasture, sitting on some smooth stones under a clump of birches. "Peter is going to church with us tomorrow," she said happily. I remember just the moment she said it.

We were all eating little jam turnovers that Felicity had made for us. Felicity's turnovers were delicious. I looked at her frowning face as she reacted to the Story Girl's announcement. Licking jam from my fingers, I wondered why Felicity had to be so nasty about Peter and particularly about his going to church. She was so pretty and such a good cook. Why did she have to spoil it all by being snooty and uninteresting? Oh well, I guess no one can have it all.

All of us enjoyed our turnovers except Sara Ray. She ate hers, but she wished she hadn't. Her mother would not have approved of eating between meals.

In fact her mother would not have approved of her eating jam turnovers at all. One time when Sara Ray was feeling quite sad and glum, I asked her what she was thinking.

"I'm trying to think of something my ma hasn't forbidden," she said with a sigh.

How I wished everybody could be happy all the time. And here was Felicity sulking around because Peter was going to church, of all things.

"I'm surprised at you, Felicity King," said Cecily severely. "You ought to be glad that poor boy is going to start going to church."

"There's a great big patch on his best pair of trousers," protested Felicity.

"Well, that's better than a hole," said the Story Girl, taking a dainty bite of her turnover. "God won't notice the patch."

"No, but the Carlisle people will," retorted Felicity in a tone that implied that what the Carlisle people thought was far more important than what God thought. "And I don't believe that Peter has a decent stocking to his name. What will you feel like if he goes to church with the skin of his legs showing through the holes, Miss Smarty?"

"I'm not a bit afraid," said the Story Girl firmly. "Peter knows better than that."

"Well, all I hope is that he'll wash behind his ears," she said in a snotty tone.

"How is Pat today?" asked Cecily, trying to change the subject. Pat was a nickname for the Story Girl's cat, Paddy.

"Pat isn't a bit better. He just mopes around the kitchen," replied Sara Stanley in a worried voice. "I went out to the barn and caught a mouse and killed it. I took it in to Paddy and he wouldn't even look at it. I'm so worried. Uncle Roger says he needs a dose of castor oil, but how can I get him to take it? I mixed some powdered medicine in some milk and tried to pour it down his throat while Peter held him. Just look at the scratches I got! And the milk went everywhere except down his throat."

"Wouldn't it be awful if—if anything happened to Paddy," whispered Cecily.

"We could have a great and jolly funeral, you know," said Dan.

We looked at him in such horror that Dan hurried to apologize.

"I'd be awfully sorry myself if Pat died. But if he *did,* we'd have to give him the right kind of a funeral," he protested. "Why, Paddy just seems like one of the family."

The Story Girl finished her turnover and stretched herself out on her tummy on the grass. Putting her chin in her hands, she looked at the sky.

She was bareheaded, as usual, and her scarlet ribbon was tied around her head. It looked as though she were wearing a crown on her sleek brown curls.

"Look at that long, thin, lacy cloud up there," she said. "What does it make you think of, girls?"

"A wedding veil," said Cecily.

"That is just what it is—the wedding veil of the Proud Princess. I know a story about it. I read it in a book. Once upon a time . . . ," she began. The Story Girl's eyes grew dreamy. Her words floated away on the summer air like windblown rose petals. "There was a princess who was the most beautiful princess in the world. Kings from all lands came to try to win her for a bride. But she was as proud as she was beautiful. She laughed at all who came to propose marriage to her. When her father urged her to choose one of them as her husband, she drew herself up proudly like so . . ."

The Story Girl sprang to her feet. For a moment, we saw the Proud Princess of the old tale in all her scornful loveliness.

"The princess said, 'I will not wed until a king comes who can conquer all kings. Then I shall be the wife of the king of the world and no one will be higher than I.'

"So every king went to war to prove that he could conquer every other king, and there was a lot of bloodshed and misery. But the Proud Princess laughed and sang as she and her maidens worked on a beautiful lace veil. She meant to wear it when the king of all kings came. It was a wonderful veil, but her maidens whispered about it. They said that a man had died and a woman's heart had been broken for every stitch sewn in it.

"Just when a king thought he had conquered all the others, another would come and conquer *him*. So it went on until it didn't seem likely the Proud Princess would ever get a husband at all. But still her pride was so great that she would not yield. Everybody, except the kings who wanted to marry her, hated her for the suffering she had caused.

"One day a tall man in complete armor, with his visor down, riding on a white horse, blew his horn at the palace gate. When he said he had come to marry the princess, everyone laughed. They knew that was unlikely.

"'But I am the king who shall conquer all kings,' he said. 'You must come to my kingdom, beautiful Princess, so that I might prove it to you. Let us be married, and you and I and your father with all his court will ride to my kingdom.'

"They were married at once, but the mysterious king never lifted the visor of his armor. The Proud Princess was covered with her lovely veil. After the wedding, he lifted her onto his white horse, and they started on the long journey to his kingdom. As they traveled on and on, the skies grew dark and evening came. Just at twilight, they rode into a valley filled with graves and tombs.

"'Why have you brought me here?' she cried angrily.

"'These are the graves of all the kings I have conquered. Behold me, beautiful Princess!' he said, lifting the visor of his helmet. 'I am *Death*—the king who will conquer all kings.'

"When the Princess saw his hideous face, she shrieked and fainted. He spurred his horse, and they rode away together into the tombs. A great rainstorm broke over the valley and blotted them from sight. Very sadly her father—the old king—and the members of his court rode home without her. The Proud Princess was never seen again.

"Now long, white clouds that sweep across the sky are a reminder of what happened so long ago. The country people in the land where she lived say, 'Look, there is the wedding veil of the Proud Princess.'"

The weird spell of the story rested on us for some moments after the Story Girl was finished. We had walked with her and felt the horror that chilled the heart of the poor Proud Princess. Dan presently broke the spell.

"You see, it doesn't do to be too proud, Felicity," he remarked, giving her a poke in the ribs. "You'd better not say too much about Peter's patches."

53

Peter's Patches Go to Church

"Isn't it awful nice and holy in here?"
whispered Peter reverently. "I didn't know
church was like this. It's nice."

Chapter Five

The next Sunday, after our long discussion about Methodists and Presbyterians, Peter kept his promise to the Story Girl. He went to church with us. There was no Sunday school that day since the teachers were away. They had all gone to a special communion service at the Markdale church. Our service at Carlisle would be held in the evening. At sunset, we were waiting at Uncle Alec's front door for Peter and the Story Girl.

None of the grown-ups were going to the Carlisle church that evening. Aunt Olivia had a sick headache, and Uncle Roger stayed home with her. Aunt Janet and Uncle Alec had gone to the Markdale service.

Felicity and Cecily were wearing their new summer muslin dresses for the first time and both of them looked very pretty. They seemed to know they looked nice, especially the proud Felicity. She wore a big, droopy hat that shadowed her pretty face.

Cecily had tortured her hair with curl papers all night and a bush of wild curls surrounded her face. I thought the curls destroyed the sweetness of her small face. But, of course, I didn't say so. You couldn't convince her that the shiny smoothness of her weekday hairdo was much more becoming. Cecily always felt bad because she had not been given naturally curly hair like the other two girls. But she got the desire of her heart on Sundays.

Presently Peter and the Story Girl appeared. We were all relieved to see that Peter looked quite respectable. Although he did have a large patch on his trousers, his face was shining clean. His thick black curls were smoothly combed, and his tie was neatly tied. It was his legs that we examined carefully. At first glance, they seemed all right, but a closer look showed something unusual.

"What is the matter with your stockings, Peter?" asked Dan bluntly.

"Oh, I didn't have a pair without holes in the legs," answered Peter easily. "Ma didn't have time to darn them this week. So I put on two pairs. The holes don't come in the same places, and you'll never notice them unless you look closely."

"Have you got a penny for the collection?" demanded Felicity.

"I've got a Yankee penny. I s'pose it will do, won't it?"

I have no idea where Peter got the penny from the United States, but Felicity told him it wouldn't do at all.

"Oh, no, no. It may be all right to pass a Yankee cent on some storekeeper or an egg peddler, but it would *never* do for church," she exclaimed firmly.

"Then I'll have to go without any," said Peter. "I only get fifty cents a week, and I gave it all to Ma last night."

But Peter had to have an offering. I think Felicity might have given him one to help him out, but Dan loaned him one first, making it clear that it had to be repaid by the next week.

Uncle Roger wandered by at that moment and whistled when he saw Peter all dressed up. "What can have turned you into a churchgoer, Peter? You never paid any attention to Aunt Olivia's gentle nudges. The old argument about 'beauty talks,' I expect," he teased, looking slyly at Felicity. We didn't know what that meant, but we understood he thought Peter was going to church because of Felicity, who sniffed scornfully and tossed her head.

"It isn't my fault that he's going to church," she snapped. "It's the Story Girl's doing."

Uncle Roger sat down on the doorstep of the house and gave himself over to one of his silent laughing fits, which we all found annoying. He shook his big blonde head, rolled his eyes, and murmured.

"Not her fault! Oh Felicity, you'll be the death of me yet!" he howled with laughter.

Felicity flounced her skirt and started off indignantly. We followed, stopping to get Sara Ray at the bottom of the hill.

The Carlisle church was an old-fashioned one with a square tower covered by ivy. Tall elms shaded the church, and a graveyard surrounded it completely. Some of the old graves were directly under the church windows. We always took the corner path through the cemetery. It led us past the King plot where four generations of our relatives had been buried under the trees.

There was Great-Grandfather King's flat tombstone of rough island sandstone. It was so overgrown with ivy that we could barely read the long message that recorded his whole history. It included eight lines of an original poem written by his widow, our Great-Grandmother King. I don't think Great-Grandmother wrote very good poetry. When Felix read it, he remarked that it *looked* like poetry but didn't *sound* like it.

There, too, slept Cousin Emily, the family ghost. We were relieved to see where she lay—that she had been officially buried here in the graveyard and not in the orchard. Edith, who had kissed the poet, was buried in some foreign country far away.

There were two white marble tombstones with engraved weeping willow trees cut on them. There was one for our Uncle Felix and another for Aunt Felicity, the Story Girl's mother. Between the two graves stood a piece of red stone. The Story Girl had brought a bunch of wild violets to lay on her mother's grave. Then she read aloud the verse inscribed on the red stone between them: "'They were lovely and pleasant in their lives, and in their death they were not divided.'"

The tone of her voice brought out the beauty of that wonderful verse. It helped us to remember that Uncle Felix and Aunt Felicity had died on the same day, although they weren't in the same place when they died. The girls wiped their eyes and we boys would have too if we could have been sure no one was looking. What a great thing to say about anybody—that he was lovely and pleasant in his life! When I heard the Story Girl read it, I made a secret vow to myself that I would try to live so words like that could be said about me.

"I wish I had a family plot," said Peter rather wistfully. "I haven't *anything* you fellows have. The Craigs are just buried anywhere they happen to die."

"I'd like to be buried here when I die," said Felix. "But I hope it won't be for a good while yet," he added in a livelier tone as we moved on toward the church.

The inside of the church was as old-fashioned as the outside. It was furnished with square box pews. The pulpit was reached by a steep, narrow flight of steps. Uncle Alec's pew was at the front of the church, quite near the pulpit. Peter's appearance did not attract as much attention as we had expected. Indeed, nobody seemed to notice him at all. The lamps had not yet been lighted and the church was filled with a soft twilight and hush. Outside the sky was purple and gold and silvery green with a delicate tangle of rosy clouds above the elms.

"Isn't it awful nice and holy in here?" whispered Peter reverently. "I didn't know church was like this. It's nice."

Felicity frowned at him, and the Story Girl touched him with her foot to remind him that he must not talk out loud in the service. From then on he behaved perfectly. But when the sermon was over and the offering was being taken, he made a commotion that we would never forget.

Elder Frewen, a tall, pale man with long, sandy side-whiskers, appeared at the end of our pew with the offering plate. We knew Elder Frewen quite well and liked him. He was Aunt Janet's cousin and often visited her. The contrast of his carefree ways during the week and his soberness on Sundays always struck us as funny. It seemed to strike Peter that way too, for as he dropped his penny into the plate—he laughed out loud!

Everybody looked at our pew. I have always wondered why Felicity did not just die of embarrassment on the spot. The Story Girl turned white, and Cecily turned red. As for poor Peter, the shame on his face was awful. He never lifted his head for the rest of the service. Afterward he followed us down the aisle and across the graveyard like a beaten dog. None of us uttered a word until we reached the road. Then Felicity broke the tense silence by remarking to the Story Girl, "I told you so!"

The Story Girl made no response. Peter sidled up to her.

"I'm awful sorry," he said sadly. "I never meant to laugh. It just happened before I could stop myself. It was just the way . . ."

"Don't ever speak to me again, Peter Craig," said the Story Girl in a cold, furious voice. "Go and be a Methodist—or a Mohammedan—or *anything*! I don't care what you are! You have *humiliated* me!"

She marched off with Sara Ray. Peter dropped back to walk with us, a frightened look on his face. "What is it I've done to her?" he whispered. "What does that big word . . . humil . . . mean?"

"Oh, never mind," I said crossly, for I felt that Peter *had* disgraced us. "She's just mad—and no wonder. Whatever made you act so crazy, Peter?"

"Well . . . I didn't mean to. And to tell the truth, I wanted to laugh twice before that and *didn't*. It was rememberin' the Story Girl's stories that tickled me. I don't think it's fair for her to be mad at all. She shouldn't tell me stories about people if she don't want me to laugh when I see them.

"When I looked at Samuel Ward, I thought of him getting up in the meeting one night and praying that he might be guided in his 'upsetting and down-rising.' I remembered that and I wanted to laugh. And then I looked at the pulpit and thought of the story she told once about the old Scottish minister who was too fat to get in through the door of the pulpit. I could just see him having to jump over the door. And then he whispered to the other minister so that everybody could hear: 'This pulpit door was made for speerits.' I was dyin' to laugh.

"And then Mr. Frewen come, and I thought of her story about his side-whiskers. How when his first wife died of inflammation of the lungs, he went courting Celia Ward. And how Celia told him she wouldn't marry him unless he shaved them whiskers off. And he wouldn't, just to be stubborn. And how one day one side of his whiskers caught fire when he was burning brush. Everyone thought he'd have to shave 'em off. But he didn't and just went 'round with one side of his whiskers gone 'til the burned ones grew out. And then Miss Celia give in and took him, because she saw there was no hope of him *ever* changin'.

"I just remembered that story when he came to our pew to take up the collection. I could just see him with one long side of whiskers, and the laugh just laughed itself before I could help it."

We all exploded with laughter on the spot, much to the horror of Mrs. Abraham Ward who was just driving past. She came the next day and told Aunt Janet that we were "acting like little heathens" on the road going home from church. We knew people should act decently in church. But just like Peter, our laughs "had just laughed themselves."

Even Felicity laughed. Felicity was not nearly as angry with Peter as we expected. She even walked beside him and let him carry her Bible. They talked quite chummily. Perhaps she forgave him because he had proved her right over the Story Girl, making good her prediction that he would disgrace us.

"I'm going to keep on going to church," Peter said. "I like it. The sermons are more interesting than I thought, and I like the singing. I just need to make up my mind whether I should be a Presbyterian or a Methodist. I suppose I might ask the minister about it."

"Oh no, don't do that," said Felicity in alarm. "Ministers wouldn't want to be bothered with such questions."

"Why not? What are ministers for if they ain't to tell people how to get to heaven?"

"Oh well, it's all right for grown-ups to ask them things, of course. But it isn't respectful for little boys—especially *hired boys*."

"I don't see why. But anyhow, I s'pose it wouldn't be much use. If he was a Presbyterian minister, he'd say I ought to be a Presbyterian and if he was a Methodist, he would tell me to be a Methodist. Look Felicity, what is the difference anyway?"

"I . . . I don't know," admitted Felicity. "I suppose children can't understand such things. There must be a great deal of difference if we only knew what it was."

A Picture of God

"What does God look like?" Peter asked. It seemed that none of us had any idea.

Chapter Six

We began our walk home from the evening church service in silence, thinking our own thoughts about what we had been discussing. But soon the silence was shattered by an abrupt and startling question from Peter.

"What does God look like?" he asked. It seemed that none of us had any idea.

"The Story Girl would prob'ly know," said Cecily.

"I wish I knew," said Peter seriously. "I wish I could see a picture of God. It would make him seem a lot more real."

"I've often wondered myself what he looks like," said Felicity in a burst of confidence. Even Felicity thought deeply sometimes.

"I've seen pictures of Jesus," said Felix thoughtfully. "He looks just like a man, only better and kinder. But now that I come to think of it, I've never seen a picture of God."

"Well, if there isn't one in Toronto, there probably isn't one anywhere," said Peter with disappointment.

"I saw a picture of the devil once," he added. "It was in a book my Aunt Jane had. She got it for a prize in school. My Aunt Jane was smart."

"It couldn't have been a very good book if there was such a picture in it," said Felicity.

"It was a *real* good book. My Aunt Jane wouldn't have a book that wasn't good," retorted Peter sulkily.

He refused to discuss the subject further, which disappointed us. We had never seen a picture of the devil, and we were curious about it.

"We'll ask Peter to describe it sometime when he's in a better mood," whispered Felix.

Sara Ray turned in at her own gate, and I ran ahead to join the Story Girl. We walked up the hill together. She had recovered her calmness of mind, but she didn't mention Peter. When we reached our lane, the perfume of the orchard struck us in the face like a wave.

We could see the long rows of trees looking all soft and white in the moonshine. It seemed to us that there was something in the King orchard that was different from other orchards we had known, but we couldn't decide what it was. In later years, we understood that it wasn't just the tree blossoms that made it special. It was because the orchard blossomed the love, faith, joy, pure happiness, and sorrows of those who took care of it and walked there.

"The orchard doesn't seem like the same place by moonlight at all," said the Story Girl dreamily. "It's lovely, but it's different. When I was very small, I used to believe fairies danced in it on moonlit nights. I would like to believe it now but I can't."

"Why not?"

"Uncle Edward told me there is no such thing as fairies. I was just seven. I know he felt it was his duty to tell me. But I have never quite felt the same toward Uncle Edward since."

We waited at Uncle Alec's door for the others to catch up. Peter sulked by in the shadows, but the Story Girl's brief, bitter anger had passed.

"Wait for me, Peter," she called. She went over to him and held out her hand.

"I forgive you," she said graciously.

Felix and I thought it would really be worth-while to offend her just to be forgiven with such an adorable voice. Peter eagerly grasped her hand.

"I tell you what, Story Girl. I'm awful sorry I laughed in church, but you needn't be afraid I ever will again. No sir! I'll go to church and Sunday school regular, and I'll say my prayers every night. I want to be like the rest of you.

"And guess what? I've thought of the way my Aunt Jane used to give medicine to a cat. You mix the powder in lard and spread it on his paws and his sides. He'll lick it off, 'cause a cat can't stand being messy. If Paddy isn't any better tomorrow, that's what we'll do."

They went away together hand in hand like little children, up the lane of spruce trees that were crossed with bars of moonlight. And there was peace all over the fresh, flowery land and peace in our little hearts.

The next day, we smeared Paddy with medicated lard. Then he was kept in the barn until he had licked his fur clean. We repeated this treatment every day for a week. Pat soon got better and our minds were free to enjoy the next excitement—collecting for a school library fund.

Our teacher thought it would be good to have a library at the school. He suggested that each of the pupils should try to raise money for the project during the month of June. It would be a contest to see how much we could collect. We could either earn the money ourselves or get contributions from our friends and neighbors. The challenge really got heated between those of us living at the King homestead. Our relatives gave each of us a quarter to get us started. The rest we had to earn. Peter was handicapped at the beginning by the fact that he had no family or friends to finance him.

"If my Aunt Jane was living, she'd give me something," he remarked. "And if my father hadn't run away, he might have given me something, too. But I'm going to do the best I can anyhow. Your Aunt Olivia says I can have the job of gathering the eggs. She says I may keep the money from one egg out of every dozen I sell."

Felicity made the same deal with her mother. The Story Girl and Cecily were to be paid ten cents a week for washing dishes at home. Felix and Dan agreed to keep the gardens free from weeds. I fished for brook trout and sold them for a penny apiece.

Sara Ray was the only unhappy one among us. She had no relatives in Carlisle except her mother, and she didn't approve of the library project. Sara's mother would not give her a cent or let her earn any money. Sara felt like an outcast in our busy little circle, where each of us counted his or her cash every day like a miser.

"I'm just going to pray to God to send me some money," she announced desperately.

"I don't believe that will do any good," said Dan. "He gives lots of things, but he doesn't give money. People can earn that for themselves."

"I can't," said Sara with defiance. "I think God will take that into account."

"Don't worry, dear," said Cecily, the peace-maker. "If you can't collect any money, everybody will know it isn't your fault."

"I won't ever feel like reading a single book in the library if I can't give something to it," mourned Sara.

Dan and the girls and I were sitting in a row on Aunt Olivia's fence, watching Felix do the weeding. Even though Felix was doing a fine job, Felicity quickly informed us, "Fat boys don't like work." Felix pretended not to hear her, but I knew he had. Felix never blushes, but his ears turn red as fire when he's embarrassed. As for Felicity, she didn't say things like that just to be mean. It just never occurred to her that Felix didn't like being called fat. She was just thoughtless.

"I always feel sorry for the poor weeds," said the Story Girl dreamily. "It must be very hard to be rooted up."

"They shouldn't grow in the wrong place," snapped Felicity without mercy.

"When weeds go to heaven, I suppose they will become flowers," continued the Story Girl.

"You do think such weird things," said Felicity.

"A rich man in Toronto has a floral clock in his garden," I said. "It looks just like the face of a clock, and there are flowers in it that open at every hour, so you can always tell the time."

"Oh, I wish I had one here," exclaimed Cecily.

"What would be the use of it?" asked the Story Girl. "Nobody ever wants to know the time in a garden."

I slipped away at that point, suddenly remembering that it was time to take a dose of magic seed. I had gotten it from Billy Robinson three days before in school. Billy had told me that it would make me grow faster.

I was secretly worried, because I thought I wasn't growing. I had overheard Aunt Janet say I was going to be short, like Uncle Alec. Now I loved Uncle Alec, but I wanted to be taller than he was. So when Billy told me secretly that he had some "magic seed" that would make boys grow, I jumped at the chance. Billy was taller than any boy of his age in Carlisle. He assured me it all came from taking magic seed.

"I was a regular runt before I began taking the seeds," Billy told me. "Look at me now. I got the seeds from Peg Bowen. She's weird, you know. I wouldn't go near her again for a *bushel* of magic seed. It was an awful experience. I haven't much left, but I guess I've enough to do me 'til I'm as tall as I want to be. You must take a pinch of the seed every three hours, walking backward. You must never tell a soul you're taking it, or it won't work. I wouldn't give any of it to anyone but you."

I was deeply grateful to Billy and sorry that I had not liked him better. Billy wasn't well liked by most people, but I vowed I would *try* to like him in the future. I took the magic seed as directed, measuring myself carefully every day by a mark on the hall door. I couldn't see any growth yet, but then I had been taking it only three days. Time would tell.

One day the Story Girl had an inspiration.

"Let's go and ask the Awkward Man and Mr. Campbell for a contribution to the library fund," she said. "I am sure no one else has asked them, because nobody in Carlisle is related to them. Let's all go together, and if they give us anything, we'll divide it equally." It was daring, because both Mr. Campbell and the Awkward Man were regarded as odd characters, and Mr. Campbell was said to hate children. But we would have followed the Story Girl to our deaths. Since the next day was Saturday, we started out in the afternoon.

We took a shortcut to the Awkward Man's house at Golden Milestone, walking over a long green meadow. At first we were not getting along well with each other. Felicity was in a bad mood. She had wanted to wear her second best dress. But Aunt Janet insisted her school clothes were good enough for "mucking around on a dusty road." Then the Story Girl arrived. She was not in her *second* best dress but in her *very* best dress and hat. Her father had just sent the soft, red silk dress and the white hat covered with poppies to her from Paris. Neither Felicity nor Cecily could have worn the dress, as the color was too bright for them. But it was perfect for the Story Girl. She almost glowed from the vivid color.

"I shouldn't think you'd put on your best clothes to go begging for the library," said Felicity cuttingly.

"Aunt Olivia says that when you are going to have an important interview with a man, you ought to look your best," said the Story Girl. She gave her skirt a swirl and enjoyed the effect. Felicity was not happy that the Story Girl was getting our attention with her new outfit. In fact, it almost ruined our afternoon.

The Mystery of the Golden Milestone

The house was a big, weathered, gray home overgrown with vines and climbing roses, which gave it an old-fashioned charm. One of the three square windows upstairs seemed to be winking at us in a friendly way through the vines.

Chapter Seven

"A unt Olivia spoils you," said Felicity, continuing her snit with the Story Girl.

"She doesn't either, Felicity King! Aunt Olivia is just sweet. She always kisses me good night, and your mother *never* kisses you."

"My mother doesn't like to kiss us in public," retorted Felicity. "But she gives us pie for dinner every day."

"So does Aunt Olivia."

"Yes, but look at the difference in the size of the pieces! And Aunt Olivia only gives you skim milk. My mother gives us cream."

"Aunt Olivia's skim milk is as good as your mother's cream," cried the Story Girl hotly.

"Oh, girls, don't fight," said the mild-mannered Cecily. "It's such a nice day, and we'll have a good time if you don't spoil it by fighting."

"We're *not* fighting," said Felicity. "And I like Aunt Olivia. But my mother is just as good as she is. So there!"

"Of course, Aunt Janet is wonderful," agreed the Story Girl. They smiled at each other. Felicity and the Story Girl were really quite fond of each other. However, sometimes a bit of the friction that was just under the surface would come bubbling to the top.

Felix, anxious to change the subject, said, "What about that story you said you'd tell us about the Awkward Man? I'd like to hear it."

"All right," agreed the Story Girl. "I don't know the whole story. But I'll tell you all I can. I call it *The Mystery of Golden Milestone*."

"Oh, I don't believe that story is true," said Felicity. "Mother says Mrs. Griggs makes things up."

"Yes, but I don't believe she could ever think of such a thing herself. It must be true," said the Story Girl. "Anyway, this is the story, boys. You know, the Awkward Man has lived alone ever since his mother died, ten years ago. Abel Griggs is his hired man. He and his wife live in a little house down the Awkward Man's lane. Mrs. Griggs makes his bread and cleans up his house now and then. She says he keeps it very neat. Until last fall there was one room she had never seen. It was always locked—the west one looking out over his garden. One day last fall, the Awkward Man went to Summerside, and Mrs. Griggs scrubbed his kitchen. Then she went through the whole house and tried the door of the west room. Mrs. Griggs is a *very* curious woman. Uncle Roger says women have too much curiosity for their own good. But Mrs. Griggs has more. She expected to find the door locked as usual, but it wasn't. She opened it, went in, and what do you suppose she found?"

"Something like—like Bluebeard's chamber?" suggested Felix with a grin.

"Oh, no, *no*! Nothing like that could happen on Prince Edward Island. There weren't any beautiful wives hanging up by their hair all round the walls. I don't believe Mrs. Griggs could have been much more surprised, though, if there were.

"The room had never been furnished in his mother's time, but now it was quite elegant. Mrs. Griggs says she never saw a room like it in a country farmhouse. It was a bedroom and sitting room combined. The floor was covered with a carpet like green velvet. There were fine lace curtains at the windows and beautiful pictures on the walls. She says she doesn't know when or how the lovely furniture was brought in.

"There was a little white bed, a dressing table, and a bookcase full of interesting books. A comfortable rocking chair had a small stand beside it with a sewing basket on it. And a colored photograph of a young woman was on top of the bookcase. Mrs. Griggs says she didn't know who the girl in the picture was—only that she was very pretty.

"But the most amazing thing of all was that *a woman's dress* was hanging over the chair by the table. Mrs. Griggs says it couldn't have belonged to Jasper Dale's mother. She never wore anything but cotton print dresses all her life. This dress was a *pale blue silk*. Besides that, a pair of blue satin slippers lay on the floor beside it—*high-heeled slippers*. And on the flyleaves of all the books, the name 'Alice' was written. Now there was never an Alice in the Dale family, and nobody ever heard of the Awkward Man having a sweetheart. Now isn't that a lovely mystery?"

"It's a pretty weird story," said Felix. "I wonder if it's true?"

"I intend to find out," said the Story Girl. "I'm going to get acquainted with the Awkward Man sometime, and then I'll learn about his Alice-secret."

"I don't see how you'll ever get acquainted with him," said Felicity. "He never goes anywhere except to church. He just stays home and reads books when he isn't working. Mother says he is a perfect hermit."

"I'll manage it somehow," said the Story Girl, and we had no doubt that she would. "But I must wait 'til I'm a little older. He wouldn't tell the secret of the west room to a little girl. And I mustn't wait 'til I'm *too* old, for he is frightened of grown-up girls. He thinks they laugh at his awkwardness. I know I will like him. He has such a nice face, even if he is awkward. He looks like a man you could tell things to."

"Well, I'd like a man who could move around without falling over his own feet," said Felicity. "And then the look of him! Uncle Roger says he is long, lank, and lean."

"Things always sound worse than they are when Uncle Roger says them," said the Story Girl. "Uncle Edward says Jasper Dale is a clever man, and it's a great pity he wasn't able to finish his college course. He went to college two years, you know. Then his father died, and he stayed home with his mother because she was sickly. I call him a hero. I wonder if it is true that he writes poetry. Mrs. Griggs says it is. She says she has seen him writing in a brown book. She said she couldn't get near enough to read it, but she knew it was poetry by the shape of it."

"Very likely. If that blue silk dress story is true, I'd believe *anything* of him," said Felicity.

We were near Golden Milestone now. The house was a big, weathered, gray home. It was overgrown with vines and climbing roses, which gave it an old-fashioned charm. One of the three square windows upstairs seemed to be winking at us in a friendly way through the vines. At least that's what the Story Girl said. We could see that for ourselves after she pointed it out.

We didn't get into the house, however. We met the Awkward Man in his yard, and he gave us a quarter apiece for our library. He didn't seem awkward or shy, but then we were only children. He was probably different around adults.

He was a tall, slender man who didn't look like he was forty years old. His forehead was not wrinkled, and he had no gray hair. We noticed his dark blue eyes and his large hands and feet. I am afraid we stared at him rather rudely while the Story Girl talked to him.

When we went away, we compared notes and found that we all liked him. We thought he was kind, even though he said little and seemed glad to get rid of us.

"He gave us money like a gentleman," said the Story Girl. "He didn't give it grudgingly either. And now for Mr. Campbell. It was on *his* account that I put on my red silk dress. I don't suppose the Awkward Man noticed it at all, but Mr. Campbell will I'm sure."

The rest of us did not share the Story Girl's enthusiasm regarding our call on Mr. Campbell. We secretly dreaded it. Who knew how he might treat us if he really hated children?

Mr. Campbell was a rich, retired farmer who took life easy. He had visited New York, Boston, and Montreal and had even been as far as the Pacific coast. Therefore he was thought of in Carlisle as a much-traveled man. He was known to be well read and intelligent. But it was also known that Mr. Campbell was not always in a good humor. If he liked you, there was nothing he wouldn't do for you. If he disliked you—well, he let you know it. We had the impression that Mr. Campbell might be like the famous little girl with the curl in the middle of her forehead. "When he was good, he was very, very good; but when he was bad, he was horrid." We wondered if this would be one of his horrid days.

"He can't do anything to us, you know," said the Story Girl. "He may be rude, but that won't hurt anyone but himself."

"Hard words break no bones," observed Felix.

"But they hurt your feelings. I'm afraid of Mr. Campbell," said the timid Cecily.

"Perhaps we'd better give up and go home," suggested Dan.

"You can go home if you like," said the Story Girl scornfully. "But *I* am going to see Mr. Campbell. I know I can manage him. Just keep *this* in mind. If I have to go alone and he gives me anything, I'll keep it all for my own collection."

That settled it. We were not going to let the Story Girl get ahead of us in collecting.

Mr. Campbell's housekeeper ushered us into his parlor and left us. Soon Mr. Campbell himself was standing in the doorway, looking us over. We took heart. It seemed to be one of his better days, for there was a quizzical smile on his broad, clean-shaven face. Mr. Campbell was a tall man with a huge head, and lots of thick, gray-streaked black hair. He had big black eyes with many wrinkles around them and a thin, firm mouth. We thought he was handsome for an old man.

He looked us over with indifference until he noticed the Story Girl leaning back in an armchair. Then a spark flashed in his dark eyes.

"Are you from the Sunday school?" he asked.

"No. We have come to ask a favor of you," said the Story Girl.

The magic of her voice worked its magic on Mr. Campbell, just as it had on the others. He came in, sat down, hooked his thumb into his vest pocket, and smiled at her.

"What is it?" he asked.

"We are collecting for our school library, and we have called to ask you for a contribution," she replied.

"Why should *I* contribute to your school library?" demanded Mr. Campbell.

We all looked at each other. Why should he, indeed? But the Story Girl was equal to the question. Leaning forward in a bewitching way with a smile, she answered, "Because a lady is asking you to do so."

Mr. Campbell chuckled. "The best of all reasons," he said. "But see here, my dear young lady. I'm an old miser, as you may have heard. I *hate* to part with my money, even for a good reason. And I *never* part with any of it unless I am to receive some good from it. Now what earthly good could I get from your tiny school library? None whatever. But I have heard from my housekeeper's son that you tell great stories. Tell me one here and now. I'll pay you according to how well you entertain me. Come now and do your best."

There was a mockery in his tone that put the Story Girl on guard instantly. She sprang to her feet, an amazing change coming over her. Her eyes flashed and burned, and crimson spots glowed in her cheeks.

"I shall tell you the story of the Sherman girls and how Betty Sherman won a husband," she said.

We gasped. Was the Story Girl crazy? Or had she forgotten that Betty Sherman was Mr. Campbell's own great-grandmother and her way of winning a husband had not been exactly proper?

How Betty Sherman
Won a Husband

*"There are lots of girls who would gladly say
'yes' to you. And here stands one," she said
boldly, looking adorable and cute.*

Chapter Eight

We were all staring at the Story Girl, wondering what she *possibly* could be thinking. What could she tell Mr. Campbell about this story that he didn't already know?

Mr. Campbell chuckled again. "An excellent test," he said. "If you can amuse *me* with that story, you must be a wonder. I've heard it so often that it has no more interest for me than the alphabet."

"One cold winter day, eighty years ago," began the Story Girl, "Donald Fraser was sitting by the window of his new house, playing his fiddle, and looking out over the white frozen bay. It was bitter cold and a storm was coming. But storm or no storm, Donald planned to go over the ice that evening to see Nancy Sherman.

"Donald was thinking of her as he played the old song 'Annie Laurie.' *Nancy is more beautiful than the lady in the song,* Donald thought. He hummed along, thinking the words as he played. *Her face is the fairest that ever the sun shone on.* And oh, he thought so, too!

"He didn't know whether Nancy loved him or not. He was only one of her many boyfriends. But he knew that if she would not become his wife, he would never marry another. He had even built his new house with her in mind! So Donald sat there and dreamed of her as he played sweet old love songs on his fiddle.

"While he was playing, a sleigh drove up to the door. Peering out into the storm, Donald recognized his neighbor Neil Campbell, another of Nancy's boyfriends. Donald was not especially glad to see Neil, but he invited him in out of the storm. He supposed this neighbor was on his way to visit Nancy that night. He knew that Nancy's father wanted Neil to marry her, because he was a rich man. He had much more money than Donald.

"But Donald was a smart man. He never let on all that he knew. He gave Neil a hearty welcome, a warm drink, and seated him close to the fire.

"'You look cold, Neil,' said Donald. 'Pull up close to the fire, and tell me all the news from over your way.'

"Neil had plenty of news to tell. The warm drink and the cozy fire loosened his tongue. He began telling Donald things he should have kept to himself. Finally he told Donald that he was on his way across the bay to ask Nancy Sherman to marry him. This was something of a shock to Donald. Although he knew Neil had been courting Nancy, he never dreamed Neil was serious enough to propose marriage so soon.

"Donald didn't know what to do. Sometimes Nancy acted like she loved him. But he was afraid that if Neil was first to ask for her hand in marriage, she would accept his offer. Her father would see to it. *What should I do?* He wondered. Then he remembered that all was fair in love and war. So he talked Neil into staying awhile longer—after all, there was a storm coming. He kept giving him warm drinks and building the roaring fire. Neil was becoming drowsy, and soon his head dropped down on his chest. He was fast asleep.

"Now Donald knew his horse, Black Dan, wouldn't carry him safely over the ice on such a night. Black Dan was skittish, especially in a blizzard. But he also knew that Neil had come in his rich and fancy sleigh. As soon as Donald was sure Neil was asleep, he put on his cap and overcoat and went outside into the storm. Untying Neil's horse from the hitching post, he hitched it back up to Neil's sleigh. Then, climbing in, he tucked Neil's buffalo robe about himself and took off. Away he went in the borrowed sleigh, flying over the ice like a deer.

"When Donald reached the Sherman home, his heart was thumping loudly in his chest. What if Nancy wouldn't have him? He would look like a fool. He found her out in the barn milking the cow.

Once again, he noticed her great beauty—hair like spun gold silk and eyes as blue as the gulf water when the sun breaks through the clouds after a storm. Standing there, he determined to have her for his wife.

"'Nan, I love you,' he said, walking over to her and looking into her eyes. 'I know I'm not worthy of you, but if true love could make a man worthy, then I am! I know this is a bit sudden, but will you have me for your husband? I can't live without you any longer. No one will ever love you as I do,' he begged.

"Nancy didn't *say* she would have him. She just *looked* it and Donald kissed her right there in the barn beside the cow. As soon as Nancy said yes, they told her parents. At first, they seemed disappointed that she would marry such a poor man as Donald. But when they saw that Donald and Nancy were really in love, they gave their blessing.

"The storm by now was too fierce for Donald to return home. So he was persuaded by Nancy's parents to spend the night in their spare room. To tell the truth, he wasn't anxious to go back and meet up with Neil Campbell, whose sleigh and girl he had stolen.

"The next morning Donald persuaded Nancy to go with him to another little village to announce their engagement to some friends. Half an hour after they left, Neil Campbell rushed into the Sherman kitchen. No one was there but Betty Sherman, Nancy's sister.

Betty was not afraid of Neil, even though he was mighty angry. She simply wasn't the type to be afraid of anyone. And Betty was very beautiful herself, with hair as brown as October nuts. She had black eyes and crimson cheeks. And she had always been in love with Neil Campbell.

"'Good morning, Mr. Campbell,' Betty said with a toss of her pretty head. 'It's early for you to be out this morning. I see you are riding Black Dan, Donald Fraser's horse. I guess you must have exchanged your horse and sleigh with him last night. Such a time we had here with Mr. Fraser. He and my sister are to be married soon. It was all settled last night. They have already gone over to the village to announce their engagement and make some arrangements.'

"'I'll be making "arrangements" for him when I find him,' said Neil, shaking his fist. 'He's made me the laughing stock of the countryside. He's taken my sleigh and my girl. He'll have another story to tell when I find him,' he grunted angrily.

"'Oh, why bother with that?' said Betty. 'Show Donald Fraser that you can win a bride as quickly as he can. There are lots of girls who would gladly say yes to you. And here stands one,' she said boldly, looking adorable and cute. 'Why not marry me, Neil Campbell? I'm just as good a catch as my sweet sister—and I could love you as well as Nan loves her Donald. Maybe even ten times better.'

"What do you suppose Neil Campbell did? Why just the thing he ought to have done. He took Betty at her word on the spot, and there was a double wedding soon after. It is said that Neil and Betty were the happiest couple in the world— even happier than Donald and Nancy. So all was well because it ended well."

The Story Girl gave a curtsy until her silk skirt swept the floor. Then she flung herself in her chair and looked at Mr. Campbell, all flushed and daring.

The story was old to us. It had once been published in a Charlottetown paper, and we had read it in Aunt Olivia's scrapbook, where the Story Girl had learned it. But we had listened with wide eyes. I have written down the bare words of the story, as she told it. But I can never reproduce the charm and color and spirit she infused into it. It was as though Donald and Neil, Nancy and Betty were there in the room with us. We saw the flashes of expression on their faces. We heard their voices, angry or tender, mocking or merry. We realized what a flirt Betty Sherman was as she made her daring offer to become Neil's wife. We had even forgotten about Mr. Campbell as we sat listening.

That gentleman, in silence, took out his wallet and gravely handed five dollars to the Story Girl. "Your story was well worth it. You are a wonder. Someday you will make the world realize it. I've been about a bit and heard some good things. But I've never enjoyed anything more than that old story I heard in my cradle. And now will you do me a favor?"

"Of course," said the delighted Story Girl.

"Recite the multiplication tables for me," he said.

We stared. Why on earth would he want her to do that? Even the Story Girl was surprised. But she began promptly and went through them to twelve times twelve. She repeated the numbers simply, but her voice changed from one tone to another as she advanced through them. We had never dreamed there was so much color in the multiplication tables. As she announced it, the fact that three times three was nine was a wonder. Five times six almost brought tears to our eyes. Eight times seven was the most tragic and frightful thing ever heard of. Twelve times twelve rang out like a trumpet call to victory.

Mr. Campbell nodded his satisfaction. "I thought you could do it," he said. "I heard someone say once that you could make the multiplication tables charming! I thought of it when I heard your story that I've heard so many times. I didn't believe it before, but I do now."

"You see," said the Story Girl as we went home, "you need never be afraid of people."

"But we are not all story girls," said Cecily.

That night we overheard Felicity talking to Cecily in their room.

"Mr. Campbell never noticed one of us except the Story Girl," she said. "But if *I* had put on *my* best dress as she did, she might not have had all the attention."

"Do you suppose you could ever do what Betty Sherman did?" asked Cecily absently.

"No, but I believe the Story Girl would," answered Felicity rather snappishly.

The Story Girl went to Charlottetown for a week in June to visit Aunt Louisa. Life seemed very colorless without her. Even Felicity admitted that it was lonesome. But three days after her leaving, Felix told us something on the way home from school that put some excitement into our lives.

"What do you think?" he said in a very serious, yet excited tone. "Jerry Cowan told me at recess this afternoon that *he has a picture of God*. He says it's at home in an old red-covered history book, and he has looked at it *often*."

To think that Jerry Cowan should have seen such a picture often! We were as deeply impressed as Felix expected us to be.

"Did he say what it was like?" asked Peter.

"No—only that it was a picture of God walking in the Garden of Eden."

"Oh," whispered Felicity. We all spoke the Great Name with reverence. "Oh—would Jerry Cowan bring it to school and let us see it?" she continued.

"I asked him that as soon as he told me," said Felix. "He said he might, but he couldn't promise. He said he'd have to ask his mother if he could bring the book to school. If she'll let him, he'll bring it tomorrow."

"Oh, I'll be almost afraid to look at it," said Sara Ray in a shaky voice.

I think we all shared her fear. Nevertheless we went to school the next day burning with curiosity— only to be disappointed. Jerry Cowan announced that he couldn't bring the red-covered book to school. But if we wanted to buy the picture outright, he would tear it out of the book and sell it to us for fifty cents.

We talked the matter over that evening in the orchard. We were all rather short of cash, having just given most of our spare change to the school library fund. But we decided we must have the picture no matter what. If we could each give about eight cents, we would have enough. Peter could give only four, but Dan gave eleven to make up the difference.

"Fifty cents is a lot for any other picture, but of course, this is different," said Dan.

"And there's a picture of Eden thrown in too, you know" added Felicity.

"Imagine selling *God's* picture," said Cecily in a shocked, awed tone.

"Nobody but a Cowan would do it, and that's a fact," said Dan.

"When we get it, we'll keep it in the family Bible," said Felicity. "That's the only proper place."

"Oh, I wonder what it will be like," breathed Cecily.

We all wondered. The next day in school, we told Jerry we were prepared to buy the picture from him. He promised to bring it to Uncle Alec's the following afternoon.

We woke up excited Saturday morning, only to have our hopes dashed when it began to rain before lunch. "What if Jerry doesn't bring the picture today because of the rain?" I suggested.

"Never fear," answered Felicity. "A Cowan would come through *anything* for fifty cents."

After lunch we all washed our faces and combed our hair. The girls put on their second best dresses, and we boys put on white collars. We felt we had to do honor to that picture as much as we possibly could. Felicity and Dan got into a small spat over something. But they stopped at once when Cecily said severely, "How *dare* you quarrel when we are going to look at a picture of God today?"

Because of the rain, we couldn't gather in the orchard to wait for Jerry. We didn't want any grown-ups around at our great moment. So we went to the loft of the barn. We could see the main road from the window and could call to Jerry to come up when he came. Sara Ray joined us, but she was pale and nervous.

"I'm afraid I did wrong to come against Ma's will. She didn't want me to come up the hill in the rain," she said miserably. "But I couldn't wait. I wanted to see the picture as soon as you did."

We waited and watched at the window. The valley was full of mist, and the rain was coming down in slanting lines against the window. As we waited, the clouds broke away and the sun came out brightly. The drops on the trees glittered like diamonds.

"I don't believe Jerry is coming," said Cecily in despair. "I suppose his mother must have thought it was dreadful, after all, to sell such a picture."

But then, we all saw him. "There he is now!" cried Dan, waving with excitement from the window.

"He's carrying a fish basket," said Felicity. "You don't suppose he would bring *that* picture in a *fish* basket."

Jerry *had* brought it in a fish basket. It was folded up in a newspaper on top of the dried herring he had just bought at the fish market. We paid him his money, but we would not open it until he was gone.

"Cecily," said Felicity in a hushed tone. "You are the best of us all. *You* open the parcel."

With trembling fingers, Cecily opened the package. We stood around, hardly breathing, as she unfolded the paper and held the picture up.

Suddenly Sara began to cry.

"Oh no! Does God look like *that?*" she wailed.

Felix and I couldn't speak. Disappointment and something worse sealed our speech. Did God really look like the stern, angry, frowning old man with the tossing hair and beard in the picture Cecily held?

"I suppose he must since that is his picture," said Dan miserably.

"He looks awfully cross," Peter said simply.

"Oh, I wish we'd never, never seen it," cried Cecily.

We all wished that too late. Our curiosity had led us into some holy place that shouldn't have been seen with human eyes. This was our punishment.

"I've had a feeling all along," wept Sara, "that it wasn't right to buy—or look—at God's picture."

As we stood there sadly, we heard flying feet below and a happy voice calling, "Felicity? Cecily? Are you up there? Where are all of you?"

The Story Girl had returned! At any other time, we would have rushed to meet her with wild joy. But now we were too crushed to move.

"What is the matter with all of you?" demanded the Story Girl, appearing at the top of the loft stairs. What have you got there?"

"A picture of God," said Cecily with a sob in her voice, "and it is so dreadful and ugly. Look!"

As the Story Girl looked, an expression of scorn came over her face.

"Surely you don't believe God looks like *that*," she said impatiently, her fine eyes flashing.

"He doesn't! He couldn't! I'm surprised at you! This is nothing but a picture of a cross old man."

Hope sprang up in our hearts, although we were not wholly convinced.

"I don't know," said Dan with doubt. "It says under the picture, "God in the Garden of Eden."

"It's *printed*."

"Well, I suppose that's what one man thought who drew the picture," answered the Story Girl. "But *he* couldn't have known any more than we do. He's never seen God either."

"It's all very well for you to say so," said Felicity, "but you don't know either. I wish I could believe God isn't like this picture."

"Well, if you don't believe me, I suppose you'll believe the minister," said the Story Girl. "Go and ask him. He's in the house this very minute. He came up with us in the buggy."

At any other time, we would not have questioned the minister about anything. But desperate cases call for desperate measures. We drew straws to see who should go and do the asking. The lot fell to Felix.

Felix waited until he saw the Reverend Marwood heading out of the house toward the buggy. The rest of us waited in the background where we could hear. The minister smiled as the small, plump boy with a pale face nervously approached him.

"Well, Felix, what is it?" asked the Reverend Marwood kindly.

"Please sir, does God really look like this?" asked Felix, holding out the picture. "We hope he doesn't, but we want to know the truth. That is why I am bothering you. Please excuse us and tell me."

The minister looked at the picture. A stern expression came into his gentle blue eyes, and he got as near to frowning, as it was possible for him to get.

"Where did you get that thing?" he demanded.

Thing! We began to breathe easier.

"We bought it from Jerry Cowan. He found it in a red-covered history book. It *says* it's God's picture," said Felix.

"It is nothing of the sort," said the Reverend Marwood indignantly.

"There is no such thing as a picture of God, Felix. No human being knows what he looks like. No human being *can* know. We should not even try to think about what he looks like. But Felix, you may be sure that God is infinitely more beautiful, loving, tender, and kind than anything we can imagine of him. Never believe anything else, my boy. As for this . . . this *sacrilege* . . . take it and burn it."

We didn't know what a sacrilege meant, but we knew that the Reverend Marwood had declared that the picture was not like God. That was enough for us. We felt as if a terrible weight had been lifted from our minds.

"I could hardly believe the Story Girl, but of course the *minister* knows," said Dan happily.

"He told me to burn it," said Felix.

"It doesn't seem reverent to do that," said Cecily. "Even if it isn't God's picture, it has his name on it."

"Then we must bury it," said the Story Girl.

"We lost fifty cents," said Felix gloomily, heading to the shed to get the shovel.

"Not a bad investment," stated the Story Girl. "We're quite a bit wiser for it."

And we were.

Lucy Maud Montgomery
1908

Lucy Maud Montgomery
1874-1942

Anne of Green Gables was the very first book that Lucy Maud Montgomery published. In all, she wrote twenty-five books.

Lucy Maud Montgomery was born on Prince Edward Island. Her family called her Maud. Before she was two years old, her mother died and she was sent to live with her mother's parents on their farm on the Island. Her grandparents were elderly and very strict. Maud lived with them for a long time.

When she was seven, her father remarried. He moved far out west to Saskatchewan, Canada, with his new wife. At age seventeen, she went to live with them, but she did not get along with her stepmother. So she returned to her grandparents.

She attended college and studied to become a teacher—just like Anne in the Avonlea series. When her grandfather died, Maud went home to be with her grandmother. Living there in the quiet of Prince Edward Island, she had plenty of time to write. It was during this time that she wrote her first book, *Anne of Green Gables*. When the book was finally accepted, it was published soon after. It was an immediate hit, and Maud began to get thousands of letters asking for more stories about Anne. She wrote *Anne of Avonlea, Chronicles of Avonlea, Anne of the Island, Anne of Windy Poplars, Anne's House of Dreams, Rainbow Valley, Anne of Ingleside*, and *Rilla of Ingleside*. She also wrote *The Story Girl* and *The Golden Road*.

When Maud was thirty-seven years old, Ewan Macdonald, the minister of the local Presbyterian Church in Canvendish, proposed marriage to her. Maud accepted and they were married. Later on they moved to Ontario where two sons, Chester and Stewart, were born to the couple.

Maud never went back to Prince Edward Island to live again. But when she died in 1942, she was buried on the Island, near the house known as Green Gables.

Measles, Mischief, and Mishaps
(Book 2)
By L.M. Montgomery,
Adapted by Barbara Davoll

As Sara Stanley continues to spin her wonderful stories, the King cousins get into a load of trouble. First, they convince their neighbor, Sara Ray, to disobey her mother and go to a magic lantern show with them. Then Sara Ray gets very sick with measles and the Story Girl thinks it is all her fault. Then Dan loses a baby he is watching. And if that's not enough, he defiantly eats poison berries and becomes very ill.

SOFTCOVER 0-310-70599-1

Available now at your local bookstore!

Zonder**kidz**.

Summer Shenanigans
(Book 3)
By L.M. Montgomery,
Adapted by Barbara Davoll

The King cousins read a dreaded prophecy about Judgment Day. When they hear a mysterious, ghostly ringing bell, they are frightened nearly out of their wits, thinking it has something to do with the end of the world. They become so frightened that the Story Girl refuses to tell any more stories. This book is filled with shenanigans and rollicking summer days as the King cousins try to make the most of their time together on Prince Edward Island.

SOFTCOVER 0-310-70600-9

Available now at your local bookstore!

Zonder**kidz**.

Ward County Public Library

We want to hear from you. Please send your
comments about this book to us in care of
zreview@zondervan.com.
Thank you.

Zonder**kidz**®

Grand Rapids, MI 49530
www.zonderkidz.com

DISCARDED